FLYER

D0171833

M.G. HIGGINS

SADDLEBACK
EDUCATIONAL PUBLISHING

red rhino
b OO k s™

Body Switch	Killer Flood
Clan Castles	The Lost House
The Code	Racer
Flyer	Sky Watchers
Fight School	Standing by Emma
The Garden Troll	Starstruck
Ghost Mountain	Stolen Treasure
The Gift	The Soldier
The Hero of Crow's Crossing	Zombies!
I Am Underdog	Zuze and the Star

With more titles on the way …

SADDLEBACK
EDUCATIONAL PUBLISHING
www.sdlback.com

ISBN-13: 978-1-62250-942-3
ISBN-10: 1-62250-942-0
eBook: 978-1-63078-172-9

Printed in Guangzhou, China
NOR/1014/CA21401612

19 18 17 16 15   1 2 3 4 5

Eric

Age: 12

Personality: quiet and kind of a loner

Family: just his dad and him

Favorite Meal: rare roast beef with garlic mashed potatoes and buttered green beans

Best Quality: determination

CHARACTERS

LEO

Age: mid-90s

Army Air Forces Nickname: Eagle Eye

Family: married for 56 years, no kids

Occupation: grocery store manager for 52 years

Best Quality: bravery

1
HAWK

There is a hawk outside the classroom window. It floats in the sky. Rises in a circle. Up. Out. Away. Weightless. Free.

Flying.

I want to know what that feels like.

"Eric," Mrs. Lund says. "Focus, please."

Head in the clouds...

I sigh. Look back at my history book. There are so many words on the page. Boring. I like the pictures, though. Soldiers in helmets. They're on small boats. They're running onto a beach. The chapter is about World War II. My great-grandfather fought in that war. I didn't know him. He died before I was born.

Mrs. Lund asks a question. The smart kids raise their hands. Not me. I turn to the next page. Look for more pictures. Planes. Oh, wow. Fighters! My heart speeds up. They're so cool. I read a caption: *P-51 Mustang*.

The Mustang

2

"A five-page report," Mrs. Lund is saying. "Due in three weeks. Any topic from the two world wars or Korea."

I hate writing reports. But not this time.

"Fighter planes," I tell my friend Todd after school. We're walking to the baseball field. "What are you going to write about?"

"U-Boats," he says.

We've reached the field. Dad is already there. He's unloading bats, balls, and helmets from the van. "Hi, Todd," he says with a smile. "Big game today. Ready?"

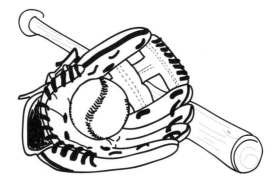

"Sure," Todd says.

"Hi, Eric," Dad says to me. He hands me a few bats. I carry them to the dugout. Dad coaches our baseball team. I'm his assistant. I wear a leg brace. So I can't play. Todd is first baseman. He's also our best hitter.

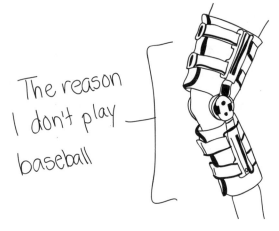

The reason I don't play baseball

The game starts. I collect balls. Pick up bats. Cheer for our guys. It kills me that I can't play. It also kills me when Dad slaps players on the back. Grins at them. "Good throw!" he shouts. "Way to hit!" "Great eye!"

Dad thinks I like baseball. That I like being his assistant. I'm afraid to tell him I don't.

Our team wins. Dad is happy. I carry equipment back to the van. We drive home. We're both quiet. Finally he says, "How was school?"

I think about my report. About the cool planes I saw in my history book. But we're already pulling into the driveway. He doesn't care about planes anyway. So I just say, "Fine."

"Mac and cheese for dinner?" he asks.

"Okay."

I head to my room. Sit at my computer. Type P-51 Mustang. *Click.* I go to link after link. Then I find an old newspaper article. It's about a guy. Leo Foster. He fought in World War II. And he *owns* a P-51. What's really great? He lives in our town. In a nursing home.

I want to see that plane.

2
MR. FOSTER

There's no ball game the next afternoon. So I take a bus to Shadow Lane Nursing Home. I walk through the front door. Cringe. The place has a sharp smell. Like pee. And strong cleaners. Yuck. I think of leaving. But that plane has been on my mind all day. I have to find out if he still has it. If I can see it.

GROSS!

I go to the counter. A lady in a nurse's uniform looks at me. "Hi there, young man. May I help you?"

"I'm here to see Leo Foster."

She raises an eyebrow. "Oh? Are you a relative?"

"No. I read about him. In an article. I'd like to talk to him."

She glances at my brace. I can tell she has more questions. But she says, "Okay. He's in the day room. Walk through those doors."

I go where she points. There are about twenty old people in a big room. Most are women. Half are in wheelchairs. There's a TV on. No one seems to be watching. A few people raise their heads as I walk by.

"Bert?" a woman waves at me. "Bert, is that you?"

I shake my head. "No, ma'am. I'm Eric. I'm looking for Leo Foster."

"What you want with him?" a guy asks. His voice is gruff. He's in a wheelchair. Looking out a window.

I stand where I can see his face. The newspaper article had a photo. This could be him. But the man in the picture had darker hair. Fewer wrinkles. "I want to talk to him about planes. Are you Mister Foster?"

"Who's asking?" the man says.

"Eric Peters."

He squints at me. Looks out the window again. "You want my autograph?"

"No. I'm doing a report on World War II planes. I read you have a P-51 Mustang. I'd like to see it."

"Search the Internet. Loads of pictures on the Internet."

"I already have. I want to see the real thing. Do you still have it?"

He shifts in his chair. Winces, as if he's in pain. "Yes." He eyes me. "Plane junkie, eh?"

I shrug.

"Nothing wrong with that. Just that I can't help you."

"Why not?"

"Why do you think?" he yells. He pounds his leg with his fist.

"Sorry," I mutter. It was a mistake to come here. A major mistake. I turn to leave.

"You're giving up pretty easy," he says. "Pilots don't give up so easy."

"I'm not a pilot."

He waves me back. "How gimpy is that leg? Can you push me?"

"I don't know. I think so."

"Well, come on, then. Meatloaf for dinner. I don't want to be late."

Meatloaf beats
mac and cheese
every time

"You mean we're going to see your plane? Right now? Where is it?"

He rolls his eyes. "You know the big field down the street? The one with a runway?"

"Yeah, but …" I sigh. I have a bad feeling about this. But I grab the handles of his wheelchair. And push.

3
HANGAR

It takes a little effort to get him going. But it's not so bad once we're moving. I roll him out of the day room. Into the lobby. The nurse who greeted me isn't there. I stop. "Should we tell someone—?"

"No!" he hisses. "Keep going."

Through those doors... FREEDOM! →

I don't move.

"Come on!" he says.

I push his chair. Figure he's not a prisoner here. At least I don't think he is. Thankfully there's a wheelchair ramp. We reach the sidewalk.

He looks around. Points right. "That way." Then yanks his hand back. "No. This way." He points left. "Hurry up! Before Derrick finds us."

Right?
Left?
Derrick???

"Who's Derrick?"

"You don't want to know."

I push him down the block. I know

exactly where the airstrip is. It's just a single runway. A few hangars. Crop dusters use it. Some people with private planes. A couple of Pipers. An old Cessna. As airports go, it's pretty lame. Even so, it's one of my favorite places. Sometimes I stand across the street. Hoping to catch sight of a plane taking off or landing.

one of my favorite spots

Ten blocks is not that far. But it is when you're pushing a guy in a wheelchair.

The sidewalk disappears. We're on the bumpy street.

"That brace slowing you down?" Mr. Foster asks.

"Yeah. A little." I grunt as the chair hits a rock.

"War injury?"

I smile. "No."

He slaps his legs. But not angry like before. "Both my knees are shot. I like to say it's a war injury. But it's arthritis."

Another three blocks. The airstrip is across the street. Good. I'm really tired. "So where is it?" I ask, pulling him to a stop.

"Where is what?"

"Your plane."

"What plane?"

I think he's joking. But then he says, "What are we doing here? Where are you taking me? Who are you?" His voice is all panicky.

Oh, great. He's losing it. I step in front of him. "My name is Eric. Everything is fine. I'll take you home. I just need to rest."

There's a wall nearby. I wheel him next to it. Sit down.

"Well? Let's go," he says.

"In a minute. Then I'll take you back."

Looks like this is as close as I'm going to get...

P51 Mustang

"Who said anything about going back?" He points across the street. At a small metal hangar. "It's right there."

"What?"

"My plane! What's wrong with you?"

I take a deep breath. I guess his mind comes and goes. I quickly wheel him across the street. Before he forgets again. The hangar is made of aluminum. It's got a curved roof. I stop in front of two metal doors. A chain is looped through the handles. It's padlocked.

"There's a bag on the back of my chair," he says. "Keys are inside."

I unzip the bag. Fumble with the keys. Man, I hope this is real. I hope this hangar isn't full of boxes of old clothes or something. At least the key works. I unfasten the chain. Pull the doors open.

And gasp.

4
COCKPIT

There *is* a plane inside the hangar. An old plane. It's small. Streamlined. Just like the pictures I saw online. The single-seat cockpit is covered with a dome of clear plastic. There's a propeller on the nose. Some paint has worn off the body. There's a little rust. But mostly it's beautiful. One of the coolest things I've ever seen.

This. Is. AWESOME!

"What do you think?" Mr. Foster asks.

I almost forgot he was there. "Awesome," I say. "Really awesome. You flew this? In World War II?"

"Yup. Well, one like it. Bought this one at an auction."

"You must be pretty old."

"Ninety-five. I think. Hard to keep track."

Wow. I can't imagine being that old. But I don't tell him that. "So, um, can I sit inside?"

He pauses. "Just don't break anything.

Climb up the back of the wing."

The wing is a little too high for me. So I pull over a stepladder. Climb up.

"Pull the canopy back," he says.

Getting inside with my brace is a little awkward. But I do it. I sit on the metal seat. The panel has a zillion dials and knobs. There are foot pedals. A joystick. I can't believe I'm sitting here. My heart beats fast. I feel myself in the sky. Like a hawk. Lighter than air. Zooming through the clouds.

"Does it still work?" I ask.

He doesn't answer. I straighten up so I can see him. His chin is resting against his chest. I guess he's asleep. I *hope* he's asleep.

"There you are!"

A guy walks into the hangar. He's wearing a white uniform. He's tall. Beefy.

Mr. Foster raises his head. "Derrick?" He looks around. "Where am I?"

Uh-oh...

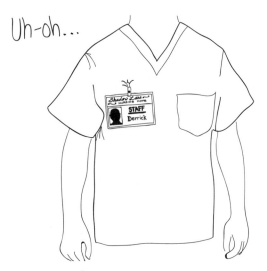

"Visiting your plane, dude."

"Is it time for meatloaf?"

"Sure. Come on."

"I'm sorry," I tell Derrick. "He said not to tell anyone."

"So you're the patient thief," Derrick says. "Yeah, that was uncool. But Leo's not

all that hard to find. Nine times out of ten he ends up here."

I hate to get out of the Mustang. I want to sit here another hour. Forever. But I scramble down.

Derrick pushes the wheelchair this time. Mr. Foster is quiet on the way back. I think maybe he's asleep again. Derrick is chatty, though. He tells me about Mr. Foster's family. Well, lack of family.

"All gone," he says. "Yeah, that plane is all he has left. And his memories. He was a famous pilot in his day. Fought in Europe. A real ace. Did he ask if you wanted his autograph?"

I nod.

Leo practicing his autograph...

Derrick snickers. "It happened once. He

got interviewed in the newspaper. A few people came to see him." He sighs. "Poor Leo. His dream was to get that plane flying again. He worked on it all the time. Then his knees went out. And his mind started to go. Now it will never happen."

"That's sad." Then I say, "Sometimes he seems okay."

"That's dementia for you. He's always a little sharper when the subject is flying."

We get back to the nursing home. I wave to Mr. Foster. "Thanks. Bye."

"Yeah. Whatever," he says.

I think I get why he's grumpy. All he has left is that plane. And a dream. A dream that will never come true.

A crazy idea comes to me.

5
IDEA

I take a deep breath. "Dad?"

He's in the living room. Watching a baseball game on TV. "What's up?"

Baseball... of course

"I want to volunteer. At Shadow Lane Nursing Home. After school. For a school project." I want him to think other kids are going. Or he might not let me do this. It's not exactly a lie. My report is a school project.

"What about baseball practice?" he says. "And games?"

"You don't need me all that much. It will just be for a while."

He's quiet a second. "Is there something I need to sign?"

"No. Not for this."

"Well. Okay. Take your phone. Call if you need me." He stares back at the TV.

I go back to my room. Feel like a jerk. Like I'm always disappointing him. Then I look at the model planes hanging from my ceiling. He bought the kits for me. For Christmas. For birthdays. But he's never helped me put one together. Not a single one.

The next day I go back to the nursing home. Mr. Foster is in the same place. Facing the window. I pull up a chair. Sit next to him.

"Good day for flying," he says. "Clear skies. Low wind." He looks at me. "What do you want?"

"I'm Eric Peters. You showed me your plane yesterday."

"I remember. I'm not an idiot."

I take a deep breath. "I want to ask you a question. Derrick said you were working on your plane. Trying to get it to fly. What kind of work does it need?"

He stares into the distance. "New rudder cables. Cockpit controls. The whole thing needs to be lubed. Checked over. Painted." His eyes narrow as he looks at me. "What's it to you?"

"I'd like to help you finish it."

He stares at me.

"It's a really cool plane," I say. "I love planes. I'd like to see it fly."

He shakes his head.

"Is it money?" I ask him. "Because my grandma left me some. I can spend it on whatever I want."

Thanks, Grandma!

"Money's not the problem. Who's going to do the work? I'm too old. You're too young."

"You can teach me. You can tell me what to do."

He seems to think. "Nope. Not that simple. Can't be done."

We could
↙ fix it!

"I thought you said pilots don't give up."

"Haven't you noticed, kid? I'm not a pilot anymore." His face sags. He looked old before. Now he looks ancient.

I can't believe this. His plane is almost

ready to fly. At least from what he said. I want to see it in the sky. I want *him* to see it in the sky. "What if I find someone to help?" I ask. "An adult. Someone who knows what they're doing."

He looks at me a long second. "I don't care. Fine. Whatever. Wheel me to the dining room, would you? Spaghetti tonight. Wait. Is it Monday?"

"Um … no. Friday."

"Fish." He makes a face. "Leave me here."

MONDAY ✓ FRIDAY ✗

6
EXPERT

I take the hangar key from Mr. Foster's bag. Leave the nursing home. My new mission? Find someone to work on his plane. So I head for home. Think about searching online. Then it hits me. The airstrip. That's where the planes are. No better place to find a plane expert.

SOMEONE around here has to know how to help!

The walk is easier not pushing a wheelchair. I stop near Mr. Foster's hangar. Feel a little nervous. I've only watched planes from across the street. This is as far as I've ever been on the property.

I look around. See a small wooden building. Could be an office. I get closer. There's a sign over the door.

I climb the stairs. Turn the knob. It's locked. I hear a noise behind me. A hangar door is open. I walk over. Stand outside. This hangar is bigger than Mr. Foster's.

Inside are a couple of planes. Crop dusters. I can tell by the spray tubes running under the wings.

"Hello?" I call.

No one answers. I step inside. Stop when I'm right under the nose of a plane. It's bright red. I reach out. Touch it.

"Hey."

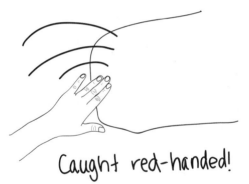

Caught red-handed!

I twist around. A guy walks toward me. He looks about my dad's age. He's wiping his hands on a rag. "Can I help you?"

"Sorry. I didn't mean—"

"That's okay." He smiles. "I don't think you hurt it any."

I decide to get right to the point. "I'm looking for someone who can fix an old plane."

He raises an eyebrow.

"In the next hangar," I say. "There's a P-51 Mustang. I know the owner. He says there's not much left to do on it. Can you help? Or do you know anyone who can?"

He stuffs the rag in his pocket. "Leo Foster's plane. Stubborn old coot. I offered to help him a few times. He never agreed. Too proud."

"Oh." I'm not sure what to say. "So, um, can you help now?"

"I don't know. I'm pretty busy."

"Do you want to take a look? I have the key."

He sighs. "Sure."

I unlock the hangar doors. He steps inside. Lets out a low whistle. "Gets me every time."

I don't say it out loud. But I agree. The Mustang takes my breath away.

He looks at me. "What's your name?"

"Eric."

"I'm Henry." He looks at the plane again. "I offered to buy it from him. When he stopped working on it. He refused. These are great show planes. Hard to come by."

"Show planes?" I ask.

"Yeah. Air shows." He walks around the

39

plane. Studies it. I follow him. "There's a show next month. In Maryvale. This plane would be perfect." He ends up back at the nose. "Yeah. I'll work on it. For free. But only if I can fly it. Can you bring Leo over? I'll need to ask him."

"I think so."

He narrows his eyes. "What's in this for you? Are you two related?"

"No. It started out as a school report. And then ... well ..."

"You saw the Mustang and fell in love with it."

I nod.

"I get it," he says.

I can tell he really does.

← I can't help it!

♡♡ P-51 MUSTANG ♡
♡

7
SECOND OPINION

It's Saturday. Eight in the morning. I'm scarfing a bowl of cereal. Henry said he'd be at the hangar at nine. I need to get to the nursing home. Talk to Mr. Foster. Push him to the airstrip. If he agrees, that is. Will he want Henry to work on his plane? I hope so.

Better eat fast. LOTS to do!

Dad walks into the kitchen. He's still in

his pj's. "You're up early," he says.

"I'm going to the nursing home."

He sits at the table. "There's a game today. I was hoping you'd help."

"Can't. Sorry."

"So what's this school project? Why a nursing home?"

I set my spoon in the bowl. Stare at the pool of milk at the bottom. I can't keep this from him anymore. "It's for a history report. World War II planes. A guy at the home owns one."

"You're doing this on your own?"

I nod.

"I thought you were with other kids. Teachers." He lets out a frustrated sigh. "Planes. I should have known." He gets to his feet. "I'm going with you today. Make sure everything is okay."

"Of course everything is okay! Why wouldn't it be?"

"Eric." He shakes his head. "You're talking to strangers. I'm your dad."

"Okay. Fine. But there's something else you need to know." I tell him about Henry. About fixing the plane.

Dad just listens. His face is blank. I have no idea what he's thinking. He looks at his watch. "The game starts at ten. Guess I'd better get dressed."

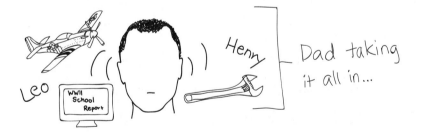

Dad drives us in his pickup. I have to admit. Not having to walk is nice. But I'm super nervous. Who knows what mood Mr. Foster will be in.

We step inside the nursing home. Dad's nose wrinkles at the smell. He talks to the nurse at the counter. She tells us Mr. Foster is in his room.

← They could use some of these...

He's sitting in his wheelchair. Watching a news program on TV. Dad introduces himself. Mr. Foster doesn't say anything. Dad steps back. "Go ahead," he says to me.

I take a deep breath. "Hi, Mister Foster. Do you remember me?"

He stares at the TV.

"It's about your plane," I say. "You said it's okay if someone fixes it. I found a guy. He says he will."

Mr. Foster sits. Stares.

I glance at Dad. He shrugs. Looks at his watch. I know he wants to leave.

Dad is ready to go...

"Mister Foster?" I ask. "Can you hear me?"

Nothing.

My heart flutters. Sinks. My dream. Mr. Foster's dream. Neither of us will see his plane fly. "Okay. Well, bye." I turn to leave.

"Henry," he says.

"What?"

"Henry," he repeats. "Is that the guy you found?"

My heart thumps. "Yes."

"Figures."

"Um. He needs to talk to you. Is right now okay?"

"Yeah. Fine. Whatever." He looks over at me. "Well, what are you waiting for? Let's get out of here."

8
AGREEMENT

I grab the handles of Mr. Foster's wheelchair. Dad steps over. "I'll do that."

"No." I shrug him off. "I've got it. You can leave if you need to."

"It's got to be eight blocks," Dad says.

"Ten blocks. I've done it before."

He shakes his head. "I'll drive. I want to meet this Henry anyway."

Dad's ride

Leo's ride

We tell the nurse where we're going. We get Mr. Foster into the cab. Then we load his wheelchair in the back of the pickup.

"So you fought in World War II?" my dad asks as he drives. He and Mr. Foster start talking about the war. About flying. I'm pretty sure Dad is just being polite. But I think it's interesting. Mr. Foster flew over France. He shot down lots of German planes. He even saved a bunch of soldiers.

We pull into the airport. I push Mr. Foster to the hangar. Henry shows up while I unlock the doors. He and Dad shake hands.

I pull a door open. Dad looks inside. "Wow." He steps over to the plane.

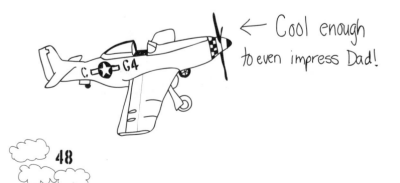

← Cool enough to even impress Dad!

"Hey, Leo," Henry says to Mr. Foster. "You're looking good."

"No I'm not," he grumbles. "I'm old. It's time to get this thing flying."

"I will. Gladly," Henry says. "But only if I can fly it."

"Fine," Mr. Foster says. "In fact, the plane's yours."

Henry's eyes widen. "Are you sure?"

"Sure I'm sure. There's one condition. The boy helps with repairs. And you teach him to fly. He wants to be a pilot. Reminds me of myself when I was his age."

Dad rushes over. "What are you talking about? No. He can't."

"Why not?" Mr. Foster asks.

"Well … his leg."

"He's got a bum leg. So what? I've got two of 'em."

49

"Well, yes. But you don't fly anymore."

"Planes can be fitted for disabilities," Henry says. "Like cars. It's done all the time."

"But he's only twelve," Dad says.

"No minimum age for lessons," Henry says.

Eric Peters: future pilot???

"Okay. It's settled," Mr. Foster says. "Write up a bill of sale. I'll sign it."

Is this really happening? I'm going to help fix the P-51? And learn to fly? I'd be screaming for joy. Except Dad is frowning.

He checks his watch for the hundredth time. "We have to go," he says. "I need to think about this."

"Sure," Henry says. "I'll get the legal papers over to Leo."

Dad insists on pushing Mr. Foster. In no time we're back at the nursing home. Then we're driving home. Dad doesn't say a word. Neither do I.

Somebody hit the

MUTE BUTTON

9
HARD WORK

We get back from the nursing home. Dad is taking a shower. I'm at my computer. Dad walks into my room. He's wearing his coaching uniform. "Eric," he says. "I've been doing a lot of thinking. I know you don't like helping with baseball. I've known it for a long time. But when you're with me, I know you're safe. I don't have to worry about you."

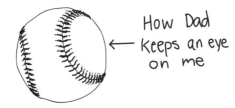

How Dad
← keeps an eye
on me

He rubs the back of his neck. "I try to

let you be independent. To do things on your own. I'm so proud of what you can do. But when I think about you flying ..." He glances at the model planes around my room. "Anything can happen up there. You're all I have."

I get what he's saying. But it doesn't make sense either. "Dad, things can happen on the ground too. I could get run over by a car. Or hit by a baseball. I want to fly. More than anything."

My DREAM!

"I know." He sighs. Taps the doorframe.

"See you later." He walks down the hall.

All this time I thought he was disappointed in me. But he was just worried. I jump up. Run to the doorway. "Dad!"

He turns.

"I can go to the game today. If you want."

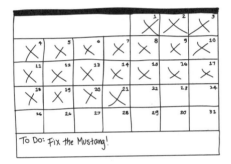

The next three weeks speed by. Most afternoons I go to the hangar. I help Henry with the plane. The work is greasy and dirty. But I love it. I'm learning so much about planes. And I feel like I'm working on a piece of history.

55

One day I bring Todd with me. He's blown away by the Mustang. It quickly spreads around school what I'm doing. Kids look at me a little differently after that.

I help Dad with ball games on the weekends. He hasn't mentioned flying lessons. I'm afraid to ask.

I've gotten so caught up in the plane. I almost forget I have a report to write. I change the topic a little. Instead of just planes, I write about pilots. Well, one pilot.

Some afternoons I go to the nursing home. Talk to Mr. Foster. That is, First Lieutenant Leo Foster, United States Army Air Forces. Some days he doesn't know who I am. Other days he does. And he shares all kinds of stories. I always feel like I'm flying with him.

I turn in my paper. Mrs. Lund gives me an A. "Excellent," she whispers when she hands it back.

After school I go to the nursing home. I want to tell Mr. Foster the good news about my report. Plus, the Mustang is almost ready to fly. The air show is this Saturday.

Right away, I know something is wrong. The nurse cries when she sees me. I run to the day room. He's not there. I run to his room. Derrick is packing Mr. Foster's things in a box.

"What's wrong?" I ask. "Where is he?"

"I'm sorry, dude," Derrick says. "I've got bad news. Leo died in his sleep."

I can't believe he's gone...

10
FLYING

All the air rushes out of me. I can't believe it. "I was just here a few days ago," I say. "He was fine."

"Stroke. It can happen sudden like that."

I wipe my eyes. I didn't even realize I was crying.

I guess I'm really going to miss him

"Hey, hey." Derrick pats my back. "He

was happy. Happier than I'd seen him in a long time."

"But he didn't see his Mustang fly."

Derrick shrugs. "I don't think that was a big deal to him. The big deal was finding it a new owner. Someone to take care of it. And he wanted to tell you his story."

Maybe that's true. But I don't care. It seems so unfair.

I storm out of the nursing home. Head for the airstrip. Find Henry in the hangar. He's touching up the paint.

The Mustang is sleek. Beautiful. The body is silver-gray. The nose is red and yellow. White stripes encircle each wing. There's a white star at the rear of the body. And one on the left wing. That's what he's painting right now.

I clear my throat.

He sees me. Smiles. "What do you think?"

"It's awesome."

Then I tell him about Mr. Foster.

He hands me the brush. "I think he'd want you to finish it."

It's early morning. The air show hasn't started yet. I've never seen so many planes. Big and small. Fancy and plain. Old and new. A few planes are taking off and landing. Giving people rides. Dad and I walk around the planes on the ground. Todd is with us. It's perfect. Like Christmas morning. I only wish Mr. Foster were here.

Henry tested the Mustang while I was at school. So I haven't seen it in the air yet. He's flying it here this morning. That's why we're in Maryvale early.

I'm gawking at a bi-plane when Dad says, "Eric. Look." He points at the sky. I hear a roaring engine. See a flash of silver. Then red. The plane zooms lower. It's like a silver hawk. Swooping. Tilting. My fingers tingle.

"Is that it?" Todd asks.

There it is!

"Yeah," I murmur. "That's it."
"Wow. It's amazing."
I agree.

Henry lands the Mustang. He taxis it near some other warplanes. We join him. His smile is a mile wide. "Flew like a dream." He climbs down. Presses his hand on my shoulder. "Thought this would be a good time to tell you. I've found a plane for your lessons."

"Lessons?" I ask.

Henry glances at my dad, who shrugs.

"Really?" I say.

Dad sighs. "Sure. I'll try not to worry. Too much."

Behind me I hear, "Eric Peters?"

I twist around. A man stands behind us. He's holding a clipboard.

"That's me," I say.

"Ready for your flight?" he asks.

"What?" I look at Dad.

He gives me a sheepish grin. "Consider it an early birthday present."

Best.
Gift.
EVER!

"No way," I mutter.

The plane rises. Up. Out. Away. Free. Weightless.

I'm flying. And I've never felt so alive.